A Day Off for Santos

Story by Tamera Bryant

Illustrations by Tom McNeely

Zaner-Bloser
The Language Arts and Reading Company

"Hey, Santos! Wait!"

Santos turned around to see Jake, running to catch up with him. "Where are you going?" Jake asked. He was almost out of breath.

"To the restaurant."

"Today? Aw, man. We wanted you to play ball with us today."

"Sorry. I have to work. Mama and Papa will be waiting for me."

"Okay." Jake sounded disappointed. "How about Friday? We're going to play on Wednesdays and Fridays."

"I'll ask," Santos said. "I'll let you know tomorrow."

"Okay. See you tomorrow."

Santos hurried off down the street toward Dos Cocinas. He wondered how he could ask for a day off. He had never asked before. Except when he was sick, he went to the restaurant every day after school.

In the restaurant's kitchen, Mama was busily chopping tomatoes. Santos could see that she had already chopped a large bowlful of onions and jalapeños. The tomatoes would go in the bowl next and then some cilantro. Mama made the best pico de gallo.

"Oh, Santito," Mama said, "good, you're here. We have a lot to do. How was school?"

"School was fine," replied Santos. "What's the special tonight?" he asked.

"Carne guisada con papas." Beef stew with potatoes.

"I hope you're making a lot of it. Everybody loves that."

Mama was still busy with her tomatoes. Santos stood watching, trying to figure out what to say next.

"What are you doing?" Mama asked. "You don't have time to just stand there."

"Can I play with my friends after school on Fridays or Wednesdays?" Santos blurted out his request. "They want me to play ball."

"No, mijo," Mama said. "I need you here."

"Just one day," Santos pleaded.

"Do you see me taking just one day? Or your papa? Don't bother me with this now. Can't you see customers are waiting?"

"Later . . ."

"No later. I need you here. This is a family business, and you are family."

Santos wanted to yell or maybe throw something. But he knew better. Instead he sulked. He took a long time to do his chores. He spilled the salt when he filled the shakers. He took his time rolling napkins around the silverware.

Maybe Mama would see that he wasn't such a big help to her at all.

But Mama did not even notice how slowly Santos worked. She was too busy cutting stew meat and adding it to the big pot on the stove. This only made Santos angrier. His frown got a little deeper. His steps got a little slower.

When Papa came in, he saw how Santos was acting.

"What's the matter with you?" he asked.

"Nothing," Santos said.

"You're moving like a slug, and you have a deep line here." Papa pointed to Santos' forehead. "You are mad about something."

"I asked Mama if I could play with my friends on Friday. She said no."

"And you want her to change her mind?"

"Yes."

"Well, acting like this is probably the best way."

Santos was embarrassed. Papa was making fun of him. "I don't care," he said.

"Oh, I see," said Papa. "You enjoy being mad."

Papa looked like he was waiting for a reply. Santos only stared at the floor. Then he went to clean off the table near the door.

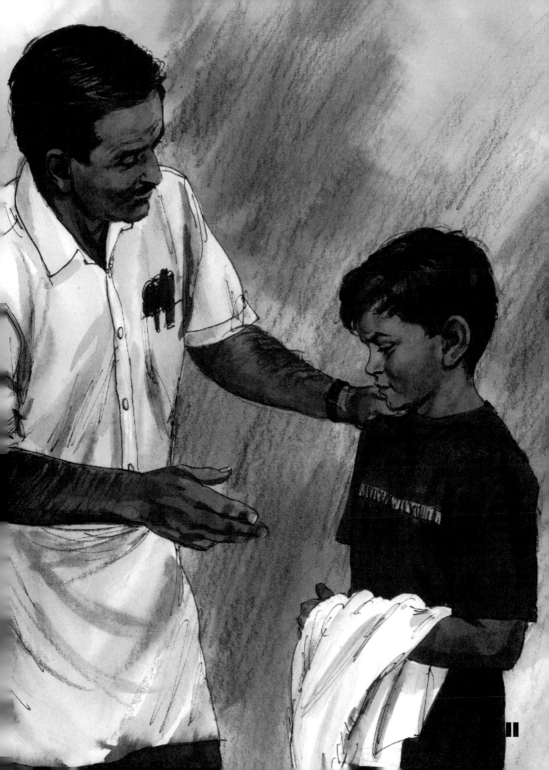

The next morning Santos was still mad
but mostly disappointed. Why did he have
to go to the restaurant every day? Why
couldn't he play with the other kids?

He thought about what Papa had said.
Acting out was not helping. If Mama even
saw him, she didn't say anything. And she
didn't change her mind, either.

That afternoon, Santos went to the restaurant just like always. Papa was already there and talking to Mama. When Santos walked in, they stopped talking.

"Santito," Mama said, "did you finish rolling the silverware last night?"

"No."

"Then that is what you do first. And then make sure the tables are clean."

"Okay," Santos answered as he went right to work. In a few minutes he wiped all the tables. The silverware basket was full.

"You are a good worker today," Mama said. "Do you want to make a deal?"

"What do you mean?"

"I have to have you here on Fridays. Fridays are busy days. You play with your friends on Wednesday."

Santos couldn't believe it. "Thank you, Mama. I'll make sure everything is done Tuesday night. I'll fill all the salt and pepper shakers and roll all the silverware. I'll sweep and mop, too."

"This is not a promise for every Wednesday. We'll see how it goes. Deal?"

"Deal. We'll see how it goes."

Santos could not keep from smiling. He would thank Papa for talking to Mama for him. Then he would work extra hard to show Mama that she had made the right decision.

Santos walked out front to greet Mr. and Mrs. Juarez. He sat them in a booth near the window.

"You look very happy today, Santos."

"Yes, I am."